W9-BFP-397

My Perfect Neighborhood

by Leah Komaiko

illustrated by Barbara Westman

Harper & Row, Publishers

My Perfect Neighborhood

Library of Congress Cataloging-in-Publication Data
Komaiko, Leah.
My perfect neighborhood / by Leah Komaiko ; illustrated by Barbara Westman.
p. cm.
Summary: A little girl takes a walk in her urban neighborhood and delights in its quirky personality.
ISBN 0-06-023287-0 : $. — ISBN 0-06-023288-9 (lib. bdg.) : $
{1. Neighborhood—Fiction. 2. Stories in rhyme.} I. Westman, Barbara, ill. II. Title.
PZ8.3.K835My 1990 89-37871
{E}—dc20 CIP
AC

Typography by Christine Kettner
1 2 3 4 5 6 7 8 9 10
First Edition

For Barbara Karlin and
Rockin' Robin Weisman
L.K.

For Arthur
B.W.

I went out for a walk today.
My neighborhood she looked okay.

753
SAM'S HOT DOGS
ICE COLD SODA

The dogs waved when the cats marched by.

LOFT FOR RENT
JOE'S HARDWARE
FISH
FRESH TODAY

The builders built a brick-cream pie

DESIGNATED
HARD
HAT
AREA
BRICK-
CREAM
PIE
PROJECT
HARD HATS
ONLY
BEST CITY
CEMENT
TEL·971-2617
BIG MAX

And clothes hung in the trees to dry.
My neighborhood's the place to try.

753

I went out for a walk today.
My neighborhood she looked okay.
The grown-ups lined up for recess.

BIG APPLE SCHOOL
SCHOOL
FAIR
SATURDAY
10 – 4
SCHOOL
FAIR
Report Card
C
B+
C–
A
B–

The poodles found a wedding dress

Hair Salon
Rita's
OPEN
TONIGHT
ding Gowns
THE CIRCUS
IS COMING!
Sat.-
Sun.
Big BAKERY
OPEN 8-9

RIGHT BANK
FAMILIES WELCOME GOOD LOANS
FLOWERS by Lisa
BIG SALE
PIZZA

And birds played bongos, more or less.
This neighborhood's the best address.

I went out for my walk today.
My neighborhood she looked okay.

QUALITY FRUITS
FRUIT MARKET
TROPICAL PRODUCTS
FREE PARKING in REAR
WHOLESALE RETAIL
LOFT FOR RENT 262-8000
633
VEGETABL
NUTS CANDY FRUITS
TEA CHINA
IMPORTED CHEESE
EGGS
SODA
UTS
UITS
3/10¢
10¢

A horse was out on roller skates.

My grandmother was lifting weights
And dishwashers were juggling plates.
I told you, this place really rates.

PIZZA
JOE'S
BODY BUILDING GYM
OPEN EVERY DAY
BW

FAMILY PRACTICE OF DENTISTRY
BRUSH DAILY for Good Health
DR BLOOMIE
CLOSED MONDAYS

I went out for my walk today
And saw the sights that came my way:
The dentist shaving someone's head,

The baker baking sweet-tooth bread,
And bed salesmen, asleep in bed.
This place is special, like I said.

46
Sweet Tooth Bakery
PEN 6-8
Happy Birthday
Sweet Tooth Bakery
BIG SALE
30-50% OFF

ANTIQUES · MIRRORS

I went out for my walk today
And saw...*myself*....I looked okay.

My legs were each a half arm high.
My elbow almost touched my thigh
And half my nose was in my eye.
Oh, what a gorgeous girl am I!

I love my walks, for then I see
That things are just as they should be.